The Magical Book

Adapted from E. Nesbit's
The Book of Beasts by Lesley Sims

Illustrated by Victor Tavares

Reading Consultant: Alison Kelly
Roehampton University

Contents

Chapter 1

A big surprise

Leo lived with his granny in a tall house in the middle of town. One day, he was in his playroom, when his granny rushed in. "The Chancellor and the Prime Minister are here to see you!" she cried.

"Me? Why?" said Leo, as she
bustled him to the drawing room.
Two men wearing long velvet
robes bowed as Leo came in.

"Sire, your great-
great-great-great-great-
grandfather has died," said
one, who was the Chancellor.
"And you're to be king!"

"But he died years ago," said
Leo, with a puzzled frown.

"He did," agreed the other man,
who was the Prime Minister. "But
ever since, the people have been
saving up to buy a crown."

"Didn't my great-however-many-grandfather have a crown?" asked Leo.

"He sold it to buy books," said the Chancellor, with a sigh. "He sold a lot of things to buy books."

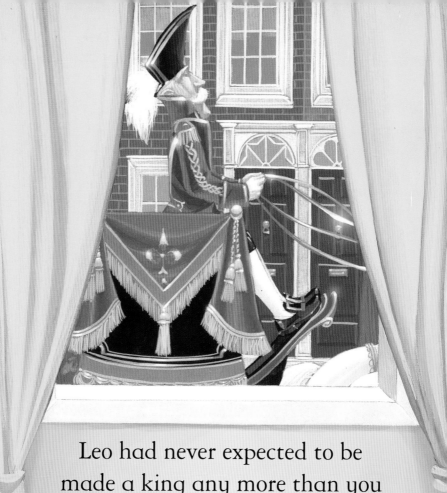

Leo had never expected to be made a king any more than you have and it was quite a shock.

"There's no time to lose," said the Chancellor and he led Leo outside to a grand coach and whisked him away.

The streets were
covered with flags and
so crowded with people cheering,
Leo couldn't see their feet.

10

The coach drew up outside a
packed cathedral. Leo jumped
from the coach, put on a robe
and went inside to be crowned.

11

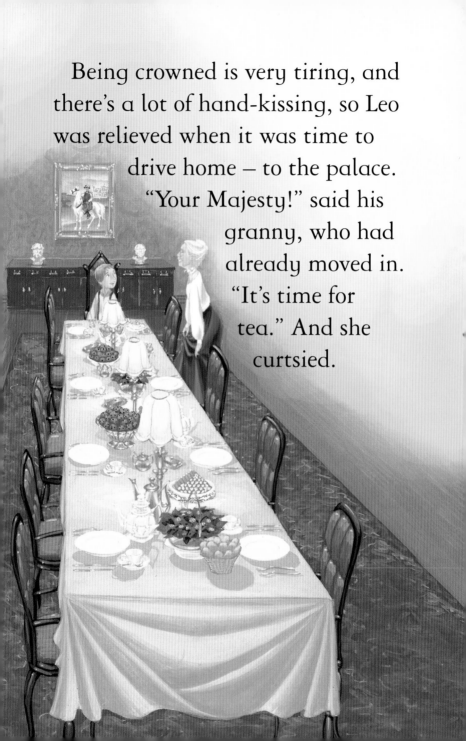

Being crowned is very tiring, and there's a lot of hand-kissing, so Leo was relieved when it was time to drive home – to the palace. "Your Majesty!" said his granny, who had already moved in. "It's time for tea." And she curtsied.

After a tea fit for a king, Leo went looking for a book to read. The palace library had more books than he had ever seen in his life.

"Who owns all these?" Leo wondered out loud.

13

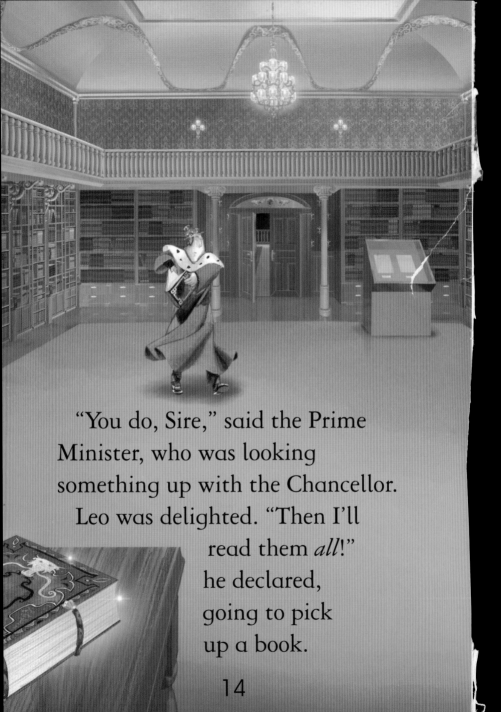

"You do, Sire," said the Prime Minister, who was looking something up with the Chancellor. Leo was delighted. "Then I'll read them *all*!" he declared, going to pick up a book.

"Stop!" shouted the
Chancellor. "Your Majesty,"
he added, quickly. "Those books
aren't, well, safe…"

"What do you mean, not safe?" said Leo. "They look just like books to me."

"The problem," explained the Prime Minister, "is that the old king was... well, some people thought he was... a wizard!"

"A wizard?" cried Leo.

"Of course he wasn't," said the Prime Minister, hastily. "But, all the same, I wouldn't touch those books."

"Like this one?" Leo asked. He had spotted a huge leather book that seemed to glow.

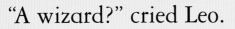

Chapter 2

The Book of Beasts

The book was set with jewels. For a second, gleaming gold letters on the cover declared *The Book of Beasts*. Then they vanished. "Especially not that one," said the Prime Minister.

But the book looked so inviting, Leo couldn't help opening it. On the first page he saw a beautifully painted butterfly. "That's lovely!" said Leo.

As he spoke, the butterfly fluttered its red and yellow wings and flew out of the book.

"It's magic!" gasped
the Chancellor.
Leo turned to the next
page and found a bluebird.
With a gentle flap
of his wings, the
bird flew from
the page.
"Enough!"
shouted the
Prime Minister.

"Just suppose the next creature had been a poisonous snake or a rampaging wolf," said the Chancellor, "and you'd set it free."

Leo blushed. "I'm sorry," he whispered.

That night
in bed Leo
couldn't stop
thinking about
the book.

"I have to look at it
again," he thought and
he crept down to the
library in the
moonlight.

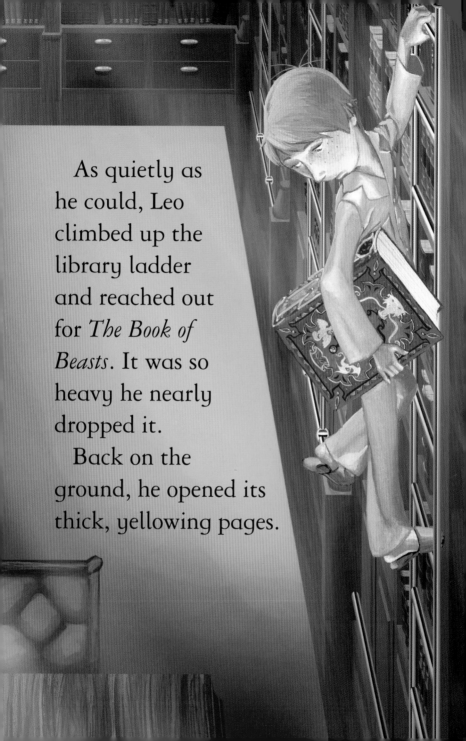

As quietly as he could, Leo climbed up the library ladder and reached out for *The Book of Beasts*. It was so heavy he nearly dropped it.

Back on the ground, he opened its thick, yellowing pages.

The first page was blank and so was the second. But on the third page was a red creature beside a palm tree, with the word *Dragon* underneath.

Leo shut the book with a bang and ran back to bed.

25

Chapter 3

Dragon on the loose!

The next morning, all Leo could think about was *The Book of Beasts*. After a quick breakfast, he took it into the garden. To his surprise, the book opened all by itself...

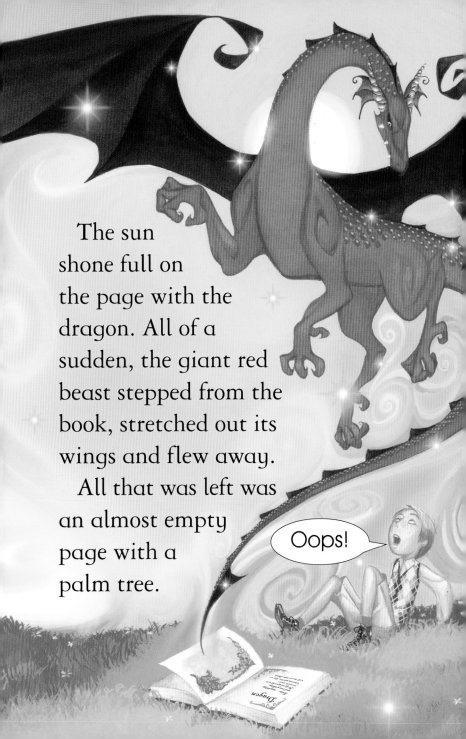

The sun shone full on the page with the dragon. All of a sudden, the giant red beast stepped from the book, stretched out its wings and flew away.

All that was left was an almost empty page with a palm tree.

Oops!

Leo began to cry.
He had only been king for
a day and already a dragon
was roaming his
country.

The Prime Minister and the
Chancellor came rushing from the
palace to see what was wrong.

When they heard what Leo had
done, they were furious.

But no one could find the dragon.

That afternoon, the dragon
whooshed down and ate a park –
swings, slide and see-saw –
and everyone in it.

On Saturday,
he gobbled up
a playing field...

...and on Sunday,
he swallowed an entire
swimming pool.

Leo was utterly miserable.
The deadly dragon was all
his fault.

33

The young king was moping in the garden when he noticed the butterfly perched on a rose. Just then, the bluebird swooped past with a cheerful chirp and Leo had an idea.

Perhaps there's a creature in the book that can catch the dragon!

Chapter 4

The Manticora

Leo dashed to the library and
fetched the book. Back in the
garden, he opened it, the tiniest bit,
to the page after the dragon page.

All he could see was the
end of a word: **cora**. He had
no idea what animal it
could be, so he called
for the Chancellor.

"What animal ends in *cora*?" Leo asked him.

"The manticora," the Chancellor replied. "I wish we had one now. He's the sworn enemy of dragons."

But the last manticora died years ago.

Leo raced to the book and threw open the manticora page. The beast took his time, but finally he crept from the book, sleepily rubbing his eyes.

"I want you to
fight a dragon!"
ordered Leo.

The manticora
gave a squeal, ran
away and hid.

The following day, the dragon
found the manticora hiding in the
Post Office. There was a scuffle
and kerfuffle among the brown
paper packages... then silence.

41

A few moments later,
the dragon strolled down
the road, spitting sparks and
manticora fur.

42

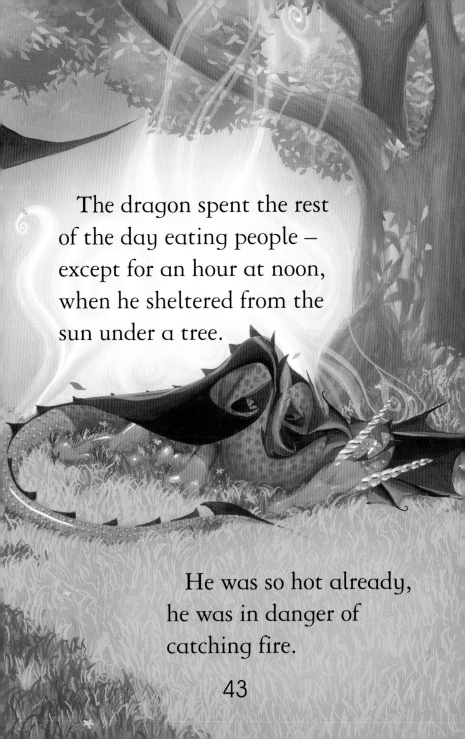

The dragon spent the rest
of the day eating people –
except for an hour at noon,
when he sheltered from the
sun under a tree.

He was so hot already,
he was in danger of
catching fire.

43

The country was in uproar.
Leo realized he would have to do
something. So he took *The Book of
Beasts* into the garden and opened
it once more.

Chapter 5

Leo to the rescue

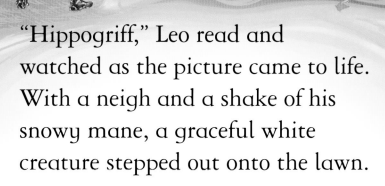

"Hippogriff," Leo read and watched as the picture came to life. With a neigh and a shake of his snowy mane, a graceful white creature stepped out onto the lawn.

45

He looked just like a horse,
except for one thing. Sticking up
from his back were two enormous,
feathery wings.

Leo went to stroke his velvety
nose and the hippogriff nuzzled
Leo's neck.

That tickles!

Suddenly, a shadow fell over the palace garden. Leo looked up. The gluttonous dragon was flying to his next meal.

They flew on and on, and on
some more, until at last, the barren
Pebbly Waste lay below them.

Suddenly, a shadow fell over the palace garden. Leo looked up. The gluttonous dragon was flying to his next meal.

"We have to distract him," Leo whispered into the hippogriff's ear. He scrambled onto the creature's smooth white back. "Fly as fast as you can to the Pebbly Waste!"

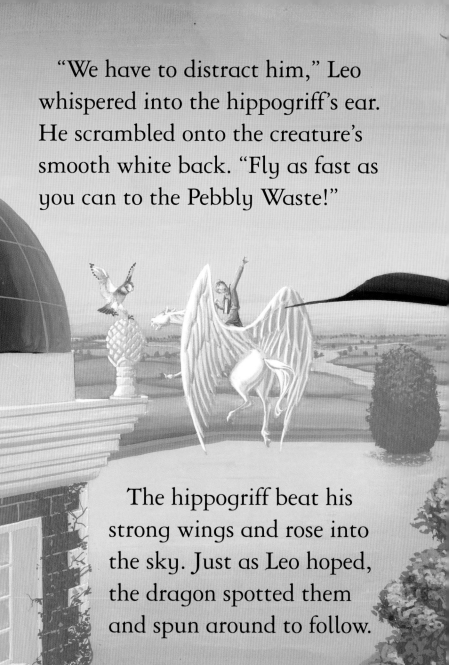

The hippogriff beat his strong wings and rose into the sky. Just as Leo hoped, the dragon spotted them and spun around to follow.

The dragon flapped his wings,
faster and faster, but no matter
how hard he tried, he couldn't
catch up with Leo and the
hippogriff.

They flew on and on, and on
some more, until at last, the barren
Pebbly Waste lay below them.

The Pebbly Waste is just like
the stoniest beach you have ever
visited – without the sea. There
are no trees. There isn't even any
grass... nothing but pebbles
stretching into the distance.

The hippogriff swooped down,
his hooves landing with a clatter
on the stones. Leo hopped off his
back, just long enough to lay
The Book of Beasts on the pebbles,
open at the dragon's page.

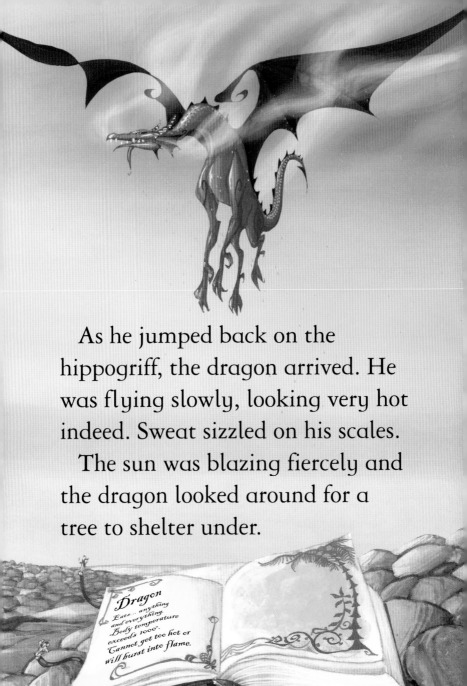

As he jumped back on the hippogriff, the dragon arrived. He was flying slowly, looking very hot indeed. Sweat sizzled on his scales.

The sun was blazing fiercely and the dragon looked around for a tree to shelter under.

Dragon
Eats... anything
and everything.
Body temperature
exceeds 1000°.
Cannot get too hot or
will burst into flame.

But the only tree he could
see was the painted palm tree
in *The Book of Beasts*.

The dragon flew onto the
pebbles and lay panting beside
the book. The sun shone hotter
than ever and the dragon's
skin began to smoke.

With a desperate roar, the dragon squeezed himself back into the book and settled under the painted palm.

Leo leaped from the hippogriff, snatched up the book and slammed it shut. "Got him!"

Holding the book tight, he turned to the hippogriff. "Dear hippogriff," he began, "you're the best and bravest, most-"

A cheer broke out and Leo turned in surprise. Standing behind him were everyone and everything the dragon had eaten.

The Pebbly Waste was crowded.
You see, the dragon could only just
fit in the book himself, so he'd had
to leave everyone else outside.

"Dear hippogriff," said Leo,
"Could you carry everyone home?"
And the hippogriff did.

Of course, it
took fifty journeys, but
everyone left behind had plenty
to do while they waited.

The manticora decided
he would rather live in
the book and crept back
to his page, carefully
avoiding the dragon.

And the
hippogriff
became a member
of the Royal Household,
carrying Leo whenever he
went on royal tours.

As for the red
and yellow butterfly and
the bluebird – they are still
fluttering and singing in the
royal garden to this day.

E. Nesbit
(1858-1924)

Edith Nesbit wrote her books a hundred years ago, when most people rode by horse not car and television hadn't been invented.

Her stories are full of excitement, adventure and magic. The original versions are much longer than **Young Reading** books, and they may seem a little old-fashioned, but they're well worth reading.

The story in this book was originally called *The Book of Beasts*. You may have been surprised by the hippogriff. This is usually a cross between a griffin (which is half eagle, half lion) and a horse, but E. Nesbit's hippogriff was simply a flying horse.

Designed by Non Figg

First published in 2007 by Usborne Publishing Ltd.,
Usborne House, 83-85 Saffron Hill, London EC1N 8RT, England.
www.usborne.com Copyright © 2007 Usborne Publishing Ltd.
Printed in China. UE. First published in America in 2007.